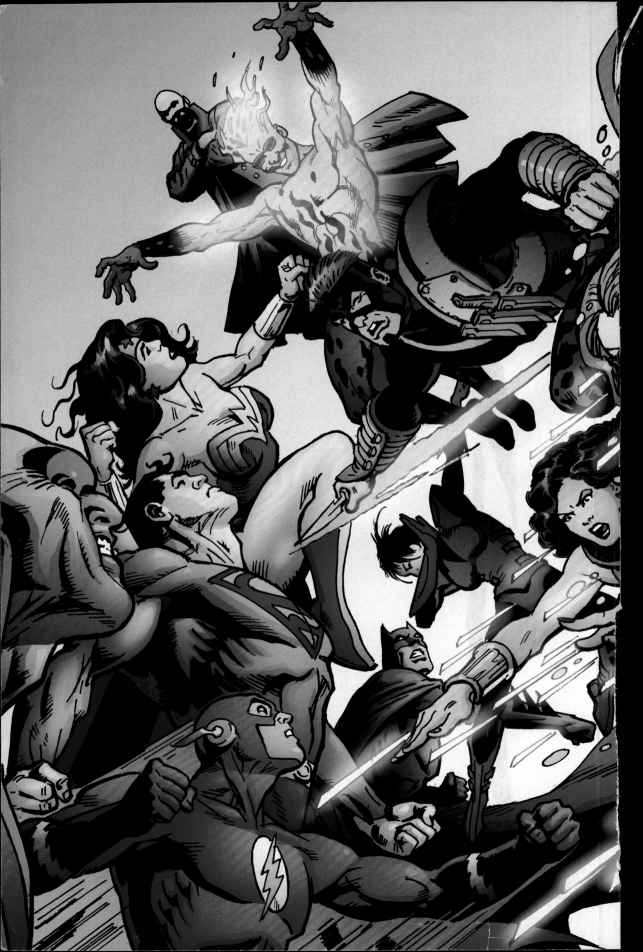

JLA

The HYPOTHETICAL WOMAN

Writer
GAIL SIMONE

Penciller
JOSÉ LUIS GARCÍA-LÓPEZ

Inkers
Klaus Janson (parts 1-3)
Sean Phillips (parts 4-6)

Colorist
David Baron

Letterers
Pat Brosseau
Rob Leigh

Original Covers
José Luis García-López with David Baron

Dan DiDio   Senior VP-Executive Editor

Mike Carlin   Editor-original series

Tom Palmer, Jr.   Associate Editor-original series

Anton Kawasaki   Editor-collected edition

Robbin Brosterman   Senior Art Director

Paul Levitz   President & Publisher

Georg Brewer   VP-Design & DC Direct Creative

Richard Bruning   Senior VP-Creative Director

Patrick Caldon   Executive VP-Finance & Operations

Chris Caramalis   VP-Finance

John Cunningham   VP-Marketing

Terri Cunningham   VP-Managing Editor

Alison Gill   VP-Manufacturing

David Hyde   VP-Publicity

Hank Kanalz   VP-General Manager, WildStorm

Jim Lee   Editorial Director-WildStorm

Paula Lowitt   Senior VP-Business & Legal Affairs

MaryEllen McLaughlin   VP-Advertising & Custom Publishing

John Nee   Senior VP-Business Development

Gregory Noveck   Senior VP-Creative Affairs

Sue Pohja   VP-Book Trade Sales

Steve Rotterdam   Senior VP-Sales & Marketing

Cheryl Rubin   Senior VP-Brand Management

Jeff Trojan   VP-Business Development, DC Direct

Bob Wayne   VP-Sales

Cover by José Luis García-López with David Baron

JLA: THE HYPOTHETICAL WOMAN

DC Comics, 1700 Broadway, New York, NY 10019
A Warner Bros. Entertainment Company
Printed in Canada. First Printing.

ISBN: 978-1-4012-1629-0

...ONLY TO SEE HIS GOOD WORKS UNDONE.

NEVER BROUGHT TO MIND

ON THE CONTRARY, GENERAL TUZIK...

...WE'RE HERE BY UNANIMOUS REQUEST OF THE UNITED NATIONS SECURITY COUNCIL. YOUR OWN EXILED SON PETITIONED FOR OUR INTERVENTION.

WE HAVE A LIST OF KNOWN ATROCITIES COMMITTED IN YOUR NAME, ON YOUR PEOPLE, GENERAL. I'D SAY YOUR BEING DEPOSED IS WELL-EARNED AND LONG OVERDUE.

YOU FILTH!

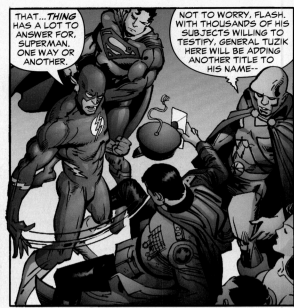

...HAVING A HARD TIME WITH THIS. WHAT'S THE POINT OF JAILING CAPTAIN COLD AND LETTING A GENOCIDAL MANIAC GO FREE?

GOT ME. LISTEN, I'VE BEEN TO A PLANET WHERE PERFORMING MUSIC IS A CAPITAL OFFENSE.

I DON'T LOOK FOR LOGIC AND REASON IN EVERY ASPECT OF THE UNIVERSE ANYMORE.

BUT IF YOU HAVE A WEAPON LIKE THIS, MY PHILOSOPHY IS...

...SAVING INNOCENT LIVES TRUMPS THE LAWS OF MAN EVERY TIME.

I DON'T KNOW WHY WE DIDN'T JUST TELEPORT THE CREEP AND SAVE DIANA THE TRIP.

FIRST, BECAUSE YOU DON'T LET A MAN LIKE TUZIK SEE YOUR HEADQUARTERS. EVER.

SECOND, AND MORE IMPORTANT...

...THERE'S ALWAYS THE SLIM HOPE WONDER WOMAN MIGHT DROP HIM ACCIDENTALLY.

WAS THAT A JOKE? DID BATMAN MAKE A JOKE JUST THEN?

FALLOUT, SUPERMAN?

ABOUT WHAT WE EXPECTED.

THEY'RE AFRAID, EVEN OUR SUPPORTERS. AFRAID THIS IS THE BEGINNING OF US TAKING A LARGER ROLE IN POLITICAL MATTERS.

DOESN'T LOOK LIKE I'LL NEED TO DO THAT, BATMAN.

DID HE JUST RUN FAST ENOUGH TO SET THE *AIR* ON FIRE?

SUPERMAN, YOU'VE GOT TO CATCH FLASH *IMMEDIATELY*. STAY *OUT* OF HIS SLIPSTREAM AND MAKE *NO* SKIN-TO-SKIN *CONTACT*.

HE'S ALREADY *OFF* THE OREGON COASTLINE.

ANY IDEA WHAT HE'S RUNNING *FROM*, BATMAN?

IF I'M RIGHT, A PLAGUE THAT COULD MAKE THE SPANISH FLU LOOK LIKE A TEA PARTY.

WE HAVE ANOTHER PROBLEM, I THINK.

I THINK YOU'RE GOING TO WANT TO HEAR WHAT THIS GENTLEMAN HAS TO *SAY*.

THE SICKNESS...

IT TOOK THE *KIDS* FIRST, MOSTLY. IT CAME ON SO BLESSED *FAST*.

MY OWN GRANDSON... THEN MOST OF THE *TOWN*... ALL WALKING, NOT SAYING A WORD...

...ALL WALKING TO *THAT PLACE*.

IF ALMOST THE ENTIRE *TOWN* IS INFECTED...

...THEN THE VIRAL DELIVERY SYSTEM IS AT LEAST PARTIALLY AIRBORNE, MOST LIKELY.

GREEN LANTERN, I'M GOING TO NEED YOU TO BE NOAH, ONLY YOUR ARK IS GOING TO HAVE TO BE HERMETICALLY SEALED, AND BIG ENOUGH TO HOLD EVERY HUMAN BEING AND MAMMAL FOR FOUR SQUARE MILES MINIMUM.

AND *YOU* HAVE TO CAUTERIZE THE WOUND.

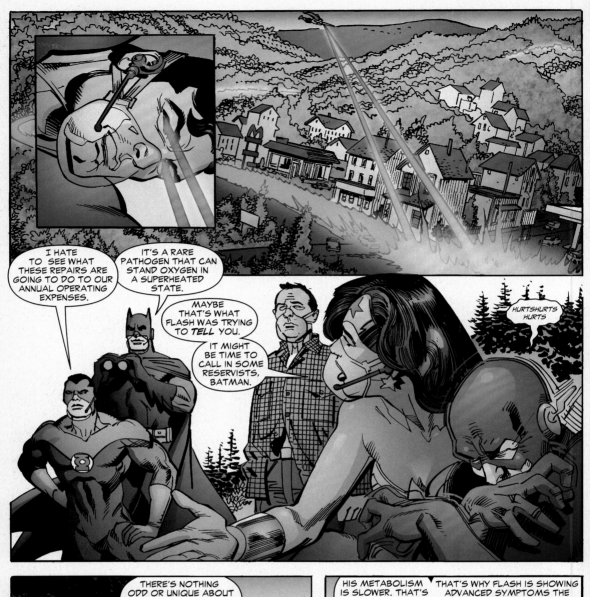

I HATE TO SEE WHAT THESE REPAIRS ARE GOING TO DO TO OUR ANNUAL OPERATING EXPENSES.

IT'S A RARE PATHOGEN THAT CAN STAND OXYGEN IN A SUPERHEATED STATE.

MAYBE THAT'S WHAT FLASH WAS TRYING TO *TELL* YOU.

IT MIGHT BE TIME TO CALL IN SOME RESERVISTS, BATMAN.

HURTSHURTS HURTS

THERE'S NOTHING ODD OR UNIQUE ABOUT THIS MAN THAT WOULD INDICATE A CAUSE FOR HIS IMMUNITY.

HE'S NOT *IMMUNE.*

HE'S *OLD.*

HIS METABOLISM IS SLOWER. THAT'S WHY THE CHILDREN WERE AFFECTED FIRST.

THAT'S WHY FLASH IS SHOWING ADVANCED SYMPTOMS THE TOWNSPEOPLE HAVEN'T BEEN HIT WITH YET.

AND YOUR RING COULDN'T DETECT THE CAUSE BECAUSE THE *SCALE* IS WRONG. WE'RE USED TO MASSIVE, AND WEREN'T THINKING MICROSCOPIC.

SCAN FLASH'S CIRCULATORY SYSTEM.

I DON'T KNOW WHAT TO LOOK FOR...

HURSTHURTS HURTSOBAD SOBAD

LOOK CLOSER.

HURTS HURTSCANTTAKE ITHURTSHURTS HURTS

MY GOD...

...HE'S FULL OF STARRO!

HELP.ME HELPMEHELPME HELP.ME!

Elsewhere...

ARE YOU PLEASED, GENERAL?

THIS IS MERELY THE FIRST CANNON FIRED, CHEN. AN ANTICIPATORY STRIKE WITH SURPRISINGLY REWARDING RESULTS.

BUT NOT MY GRAND ATTACK. SHE IS SOMETHING QUITE SPECIAL.

AND WHAT DOES SHE DO, GENERAL?

WHAT DOES SHE DO? SHE REVERSES THE NATURAL ORDER OF THE UNIVERSE. SHE COUNTERS ENTROPY. IN SHORT--

Continuing the memoirs of General Dvory Tuzik...

REGARDING THE ACCUSATION THAT I WAS AN ENTHUSIASTIC PROPONENT OF BIOLOGICAL MUNITIONS--

--I PROUDLY CONFESS THAT I HAVE USED EVERY WEAPON AT MY DISPOSAL TO DEFEND MY COUNTRY FROM ENEMIES BOTH INSIDE AND OUTSIDE ITS GLORIOUS BORDERS.

WAS I THE FIRST SUCH LEADER?

FOUR VISIBLE GUARDS ON THE GROUNDS, ONE IN THE TOWER, ERICH.

ALL RIGHT, ISAAC. SOON AS OUR SCOUT GETS BACK WITH THE RECON, CHING HAS THE TOWER.

IT IS HISTORICALLY EVIDENT THAT I WAS NOT.

IT IS BELIEVED THAT ARROWS DIPPED IN PUTREFIED ADDER VENOM AND HUMAN DUNG WERE IN COMMON USE FIVE HUNDRED YEARS BEFORE THE BIRTH OF CHRIST.

THE WORD "TOXIC" COMES FROM THE GREEK WORD "TOXICON," MEANING "ARROW," IN FACT.

THERE ARE SIX ADDITIONAL GUARDS ON THE FAR SIDE OF THE COMPOUND, CAPTAIN. THE REST MUST BE ASLEEP.

YOUR ARM, DULU?

THERE WERE DOGS.

MANY MORE EXAMPLES, BOTH STUNNING IN THEIR EFFICIENCY AND ELEGANT IN THEIR SIMPLICITY:

YOU ALL KNOW WHY WE'RE HERE, TONIGHT.

INSIDE THAT COMPOUND, SLEEPING ON SILK SHEETS, IS A MONSTER.

TUZIK IS AN ABUSER OF WOMEN, A TORTURER OF CHILDREN, A MURDERER OF VILLAGES.

WE CAN'T LET THIS MAN HAVE ANOTHER HEARTY BREAKFAST.

WE CAN'T LET HIS EXAMPLE STAND.

THE 14TH CENTURY TARTARS CATAPULTED THE BODIES OF PLAGUE VICTIMS INTO WHAT IS NOW FEODOSIA, IN THE UKRAINE.

KNOCK KNOCK KNOCK

MR. TUZIK?

(PITY THEY DIDN'T KNOW FLEAS ON VERMIN CARRIED THE PLAGUE, NOT CORPSES).

IN NORTH AMERICA, NATIVES WERE GIVEN BABY BLANKETS INFECTED WITH SMALLPOX, CHOLERA AND TUBERCULOSIS.

AFFLICTED AMERICAN AND ENGLISH SOLDIERS WERE ENCOURAGED TO COUGH AND BLEED ON THE BLANKETS. TO RUB THEM WITH THEIR OPEN WOUNDS.

IT'S TIME TO PREPARE FOR YOUR BROADCAST, MR. TUZIK.

CHEN, IF YOU'RE TO BE MY ADMINISTRATOR, I DO WISH YOU WOULD REFER TO ME BY MY WELL-EARNED MILITARY TITLE.

YOU ARE NO LONGER A GENERAL, MR. TUZIK. YOU ARE A GUEST OF MY COUNTRY.

THAT IS ALL.

YOUR COUNTRY.

YOUR COUNTRY HAS ABYSMAL FOOD AND ATROCIOUS WEATHER, BUT I WILL ADMIT...

...YOU DO SEEM TO RAISE DELIGHTFULLY ACCOMMODATING YOUNG WOMEN. NOT RELATIVES OF YOURS, I HOPE?

SO, YES, I, AND A HUNDRED LEADERS REVERED AS HEROES BY THEIR COUNTRYMEN, HAVE FOLLOWED A LONG TRADITION IN SMITING OUR ENEMIES WITH THE WEAPONS AT HAND.

HOLD THIS, PLEASE.

...

CALL ME A WAR CRIMINAL, IF YOU MUST.

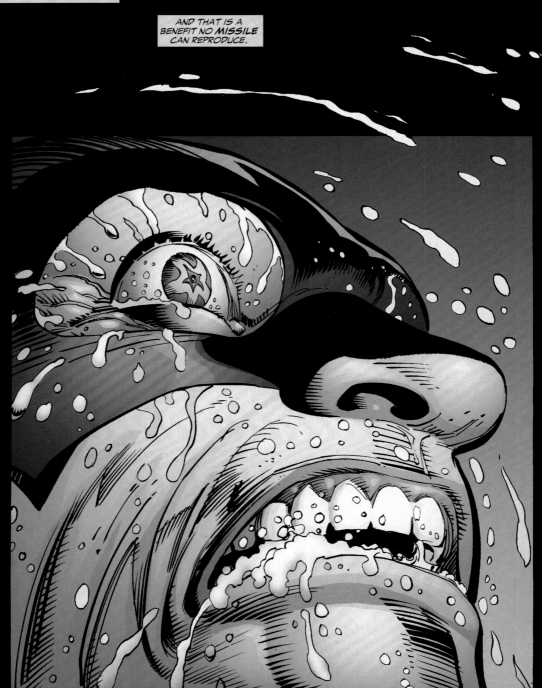

...THEY CAUSE TERROR AND **DISSENSION** IN THE RANKS OF YOUR ENEMIES.

AND THAT IS A BENEFIT NO MISSILE CAN REPRODUCE.

BLOOD IS NOT ENOUGH

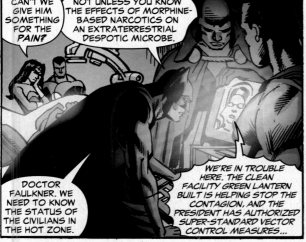

TWENTY-FIVE YEARS AGO, NO ONE HAD HEARD OF AIDS. NOW 44 MILLION ARE INFECTED. DENGUE FEVER, HANTAVIRUS...

EARTH DOESN'T NEED ANOTHER KILLER ILLNESS, BATMAN.

UNDERSTOOD, DOCTOR.

BATMAN... YOU KNOW I'VE BEEN EMPOWERED TO *QUARANTINE* THE J.L.A. AS A CONTAGION RISK IF I SEE FIT.

I KNOW ABOUT FLASH.

DR. FAULKNER, THIS IS SUPERMAN.

FLASH IS EXHIBITING ADVANCED SYMPTOMOLOGY, AND WE'RE TAKING EVERY PRECAUTION. BUT WE ARE NOT INFECTED.

I GIVE YOU MY WORD.

JLA

WELL, YOU SOUNDED MORE CONVINCING THAN I WOULD.

I MOST *SINCERELY* HOPE WE'RE *RIGHT.*

...AND THE ENTIRE JUSTICE LEAGUE WAS WITHIN THE OUTBREAK PERIMETER, IS THAT WHAT YOU'RE TELLING ME, DR. FAULKNER?

YES, MR. PRESIDENT, BUT...

AND, TO YOUR KNOWLEDGE, ARE ANY OF THE INFECTED OREGONIANS SHOWING SIGNS OF REMISSION?

NO, MR. SECRETARY. QUITE THE OPPOSITE, IN FACT.

BUT SUPERMAN *PERSONALLY* ASSURED ME THAT...

DR. FA... KITTY. WHAT IS THE PRIMARY GOAL OF THE FULL-SIZED CONQUEROR?

SUBJUGATION OF ALL SENTIENT BEINGS, SIR.

AND HOW DOES IT BRING THIS ABOUT, HISTORICALLY?

IT TAKES OVER THE BRAIN AND MOTOR FUNCTIONS OF ITS VICTIMS, MR. PRESIDENT.

THANK YOU, DOCTOR.

I DON'T WANT ANYONE TO MISUNDERSTAND WHAT I'M ABOUT TO SAY.

THIS IS NOT A MANDATE FOR ACTION AT THIS TIME.

BUT, TOM...

YES, MR. PRESIDENT?

I NEED TO KNOW WHAT WE HAVE THAT WE CAN USE TO TURN THAT MOONBASE INTO A POWDERY CRATER.

HATE TO ADD TO OUR PROBLEMS, BUT...

PEOPLE ALREADY THINK WE'RE CARRIERS.

...WHEN OUR NEWS 4 CHOPPER BRAVELY CAUGHT THIS GBS EXCLUSIVE FOOTAGE...

...A GLOWING STRUCTURE LOOKING FOR ALL THE WORLD LIKE A TEMPORARY PRISON CAMP...

...THE FRIGHTENING POSSIBILITY THE MEMBERS OF THE JUSTICE LEAGUE ARE IN FACT ALREADY INFECTED...

CITYWIDE DISASTER

...BREAKING STORY, AS THE TINY COUNTRY OF SANTA PRISCA IS EXPERIENCING WHAT SEEMS TO BE AN EPIDEMIC OF SEIZURES...

I'LL STAY WITH FLASH. SOMEONE NEEDS TO BE HERE.

DIANA, IF YOU'D PREFER THAT I STAY...

THIS TASK IS APPOINTED TO ME, J'ONN. GO.

COME ON, BATMAN.

HE'LL BE ALL RIGHT.

I KNOW SUPERMAN MEANS IT. HIS OPTIMISM IS WHAT MOST AFFECTS THE PEOPLE WHO KNOW HIM. IT STAYS WITH YOU, EVEN WHEN HE'S GONE.

BUT HE COULD BE WRONG. YOU MIGHT WELL NEVER BE "ALL RIGHT" AGAIN.

...I KNOW I CAN END YOUR LIFE TO EASE YOUR PAIN.

BE WELL, FLASH.

PLEASE BE WELL.

AND THAT'S WHY I STAYED, FLASH. THE AMAZONS ARE HEALERS, BUT WE'RE ALSO WARRIORS. WE MEASURE LIFE IN PRAGMATIC TERMS.

IF IT COMES TO IT, AND HOPE IS GONE...

Santa Prisca.

I'M ABOUT A KILOMETER FROM THE CAPITAL CITY.

I'M EXPERIENCING A HEADACHE, AND AS I GET CLOSER, IT GAINS IN INTENSITY.

WHATEVER IT IS, IT'S AFFECTING ME, AS WELL, DESPITE MY MARTIAN CELLULAR STRUCTURE.

MY VISION AND TELEPATHY SEEM PARTICULARLY IMPAIRED.

WHATEVER'S DOING THIS, IT'S FATAL TO WILDLIFE.

SUPERMAN, BE CAUTIOUS.

THERE ARE TWO MILLION PEOPLE IN THIS CITY, J'ONN--

Hmm.

SUPERMAN, CAN YOU FOCUS YOUR X-RAY VISION ON... EPICENTER OF THE PHENOMENON?

THAT'S THE MOST LIKELY SPOT FOR... TRANSMITTER.

BELAY THAT, BATMAN. AT DEPTHS OF TEN METERS, THE FISH ARE SWIMMING IN IRREGULAR PATTERNS, BUT THEY'RE ALIVE.

AT TWENTY, THEY'RE UNAFFECTED. DOESN'T TAKE AQUAMAN TO FIGURE THESE FISH OUT... THE EFFECT IS COMING FROM ABOVE.

CAN YOU TRACK THE SOURCE?

I CAN TRY. HARD TO...HARD TO CONCENTRATE.

I'LL TRY. RING'S NOT BLOCKING... THE COMPLETE EFFECT.

DO YOUR BEST, JOHN.

I'M GOING TO HELP SOME FOLKS.

BATMAN...

J'ONN...

I NEED YOU BOTH TO STAY OUTSIDE OF THE EFFECT FIELD.

I'M... AFRAID NOT... SUPERMAN.

WELL. HE'S FREE, THEN.

WRRRR

THIS MAY BE A LONG NIGHT.

‽UNHGH!‽

COMPARED TO A NORMAL MORTAL, I'M VERY, VERY FAST.

COMPARED TO ME, THE FLASH IS AN INDISTINCT BLUR.

I WONDER HOW MANY TIMES HE CAN HIT ME LIKE THAT IN A NIGHT. MILLIONS? HUNDREDS OF MILLIONS?

WRRRRRRRR

THE SCORCH MARKS...

FLASH KNOWS HOW NOT TO LEAVE THOSE. THE CONQUEROR STRAIN MUST BE COMPLETELY IN CHAR--

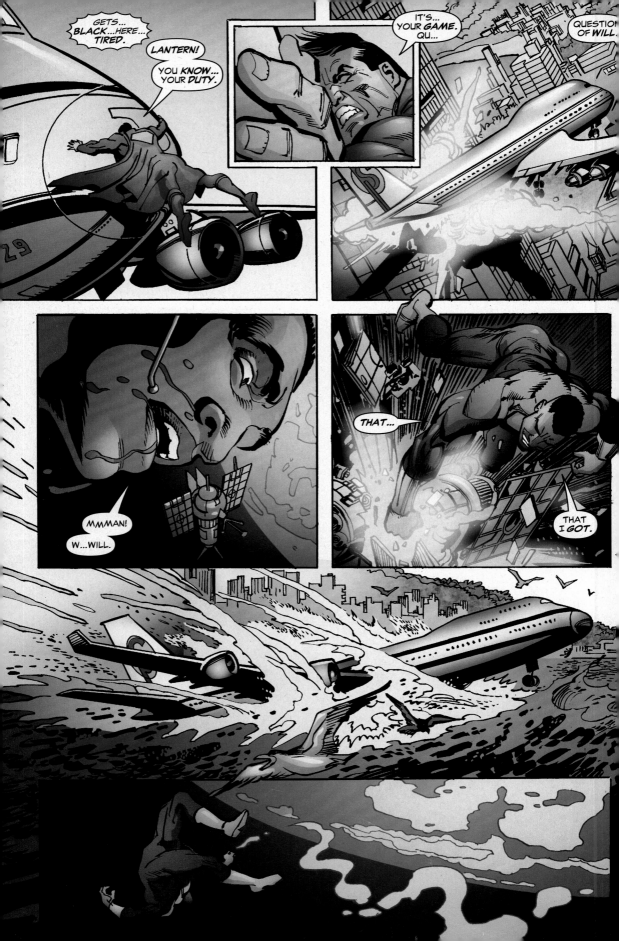

IT'S DONE, CAPTAIN. I'LL MEET YOU AT THE GATE.

EVERYONE... GO.

STOP.

LAY DOWN YOUR WEAPONS AND YOU WILL NOT BE HARMED.

OF COURSE, BIOLOGICAL WEAPONS...

I'M AFRAID THE DOGS USUALLY BARK ALL NIGHT, MY NEW FRIENDS. THEY MAKE A TERRIBLE DIN.

WHEN THEY WERE SILENT, SUSPICIONS WERE AROUSED.

...THEY'RE REALLY JUST THE APPETIZER.

NOW, THE MAIN COURSE, THE ENTREE--

I LOVE YOU, ERICH. I WISH I'D TOLD YOU BEFORE.

MARIEKA...

--THAT SHOULD ALWAYS BE SOMETHING INTERESTING.

IT SHOULD BE SOMETHING YOUR GUESTS WILL REMEMBER FOREVER.

WHAT ARE YOU GOING TO DO TO US?

YOUNG WOMAN, I'M GOING TO PUT A SINGLE BULLET IN THE HEAD OF EACH OF YOU.

AND OF COURSE, IT'S ALWAYS WISE--

--TO USE ONLY THE VERY FRESHEST INGREDIENTS.

...AND THEN, I'M GOING TO FEED YOU TO A GODDESS.

RUMORS OF COUNTRIES BIDDING VAST SUMS IN SECRET AUCTIONS...

I HAD HEARD *RUMBLINGS.*

...FOR THE DETRITUS OF BATTLES, THE TECHNOLOGICAL *SCAVENGINGS* LEFT LYING ON THE GROUND WHEN WE *THOUGHT* THE DANGER WAS OVER.

WE UNDERESTIMATED MANKIND. OR *OVER*ESTIMATED THEM.

MONEY THAT COULD HAVE GONE TO SHORING UP A CRUMBLING INFRASTRUCTURE, OR FEEDING A HUNGRY POPULATION--

--INSTEAD WENT TO BUYING THE *SCRAPS* OF TWISTED AND ANGRY INVENTIONS, IN THE SLIM HOPE OF A REVERSE-ENGINEERED MIRACLE WEAPON.

WE NEVER THOUGHT TO PICK UP AFTER OURSELVES.

FLASH IS INFECTED BY THE CONQUEROR VIRUS, AND BATMAN, GREEN LANTERN, AND WONDER WOMAN AREN'T RESPONDING TO OUR SIGNAL.

AND IT LOOKS LIKE EARTH JUST DECLARED *WAR* ON THE *JUSTICE LEAGUE*.

STEEL HEART

ARE THEY...

TAMARANEAN SHIPS, YES, OR AT LEAST, FOR THE MOST PART.

THEY CARRY SOME COMPONENTS THAT SEEM TO MIMIC THOSE IN THE SHIP THAT CRASHED IN METROPOLIS DURING THE FINAL NIGHT AFFAIR.

AND THE OTHER THREAT APPEARS TO BE BASED ON CHEMO...

THREE CHEMOS.

PERHAPS IT *IS* TIME TO CALL IN THE RESERVISTS.

CHEMO IS CAPABLE OF SPONTANEOUSLY PRODUCING THE MOST TOXIC AND CORROSIVE CHEMICAL COMPOUNDS ON EARTH, J'ONN.

WHO WOULD WE CALL? WHOSE NAME WOULD YOU PUT ON THAT LIST?

SHLIP SHLUPP THLIPP

I'M AFRAID IT'S YOU AND ME.

FORGIVE MY SUDDEN CHANGE OF APPEARANCE. A SHEDDABLE LAYER OF DERMAL ARMOR SEEMED PRUDENT.

AND I UNDERSTAND, KAL-EL. COMPLETELY.

AS ALWAYS... IT'S MY HONOR TO FIGHT WITH YOU, J'ONN.

FLASH... I DIDN'T WANT TO DO THIS.

NO. CAN'T MAKE US. CAN'T MAKE US LOOK.

BUT I'M AFRAID YOU DON'T HAVE MUCH TIME LEFT.

YOU HAVE TO BE MADE TO SEE WHAT'S INSIDE YOU.

OH. NO.

"EVEN THE RIGHTEOUS BEING CAN DOUBT THE PURITY OF HIS SOUL AT THE TOUCH OF THE LASSO."

"TO THE TAINTED, ITS REVELATIONS CAN BE AKIN TO TORTURE."

GET THEM OUT OF ME! GET THEM OUUUUTTT!

IT TURNS OUT THAT WE MIGHT HAVE UNDERESTIMATED THE THREAT OF THE *FIGHTER SHIPS.*

WE'RE DELIBERATELY KEEPING THE BATTLE IN THE AIR, TO MINIMIZE THE DAMAGE OF THE CHEMO CONSTRUCTS' *BREATH.*

THE *DOWNSIDE* IS, EVERY *BLAST* THEY FIRE AT US GETS *CLOSER* TO OUR SPECIFIC *VULNERABILITIES.*

THEY'RE *SCANNING* US, SOMEHOW.

NOT TO MENTION THAT EACH *STEP* THEY TAKE IS A POTENTIAL *CHERNOBYL.*

J'ONN! WE *LOST* THREE. THEY'RE HEADED FOR SANTA PRISCA!

-NGH.-

THIS SHOULD TEACH US NOT TO LEAVE THE BROKEN *TOYS* IN THE *YARD.*

ENOUGH.

YOU HAVE TO *ADMIRE* THE INGENUITY, REALLY.

THEY'VE MANAGED FAIR APPROXIMATIONS OF *ALIEN SCIENCE* AND ONCE-IN-A-LIFETIME *ACCIDENTS.*

FOR A GROUP FORMED AT LEAST PARTIALLY FOR WANT OF COMPANIONSHIP...THIS FEELS LIKE A RARE MOMENT.

ALL HERE, ALL INTACT, AND EVEN IF WE'RE SOMEONE'S TARGET, FOR NOW, WE'RE CONTENT.

THE RING IS SMART, BUT IT'S BIG ON FREE WILL. HAD TO COME TO ON MY OWN BEFORE IT TOOK ME BACK HERE.

YOU MISSED SOME ODD MOMENTS, G.L.

THANKS, SUPES.

SO ANYWAY, DON'T THINK THE LI'L STARROS AREN'T SMART. THEY BLOCKED MY BRAIN'S ACCESS TO THE VIBRATIONAL FREQUENCY THAT WOULD BURN THEM OUT OF MY CELLS.

'TIL WONDER WO--! HEY, WHERE IS DIANA?

I THOUGHT I'D MAKE SOME REFRESHMENTS.

IT'S A THEMYSCIRAN CONFECTION, SWEETENED WITH POMEGRANATE. MY MOTHER'S RECIPE.

WONDER WOMAN BAKED?

WE STILL HAVE A PROBLEM. J'ONN, WHAT DID YOUR TELEPATHIC SCAN REVEAL FROM THE PILOTS?

NOTHING. THEY'RE INFECTED BY THE CONQUEROR STRAIN, UNTIL WE FIGURE OUT HOW TO DO FLASH'S VIBRATIONAL EFFECT WITHOUT KILLING THE HOST BODIES.

GREEN LANTERN'S QUARANTINED THEM IN THE SICK BAY.

I'M AFRAID TO TRY IT, AND I'M AFRAID NOT TO TRY IT.

I ADMIRE CHINA. DON'T MISUNDERSTAND ME.

NO COUNTRY ON THE PLANET IS CHANGING SO RAPIDLY, YET SO...*QUIETLY.*

IN THE CITIES, IT IS NOW POSSIBLE TO WALK MANY BLOCKS AND NEVER SEE A PARTY FLAG.

THE PEOPLE EAT FRIED CHICKEN AND PIZZA AND HAMBURGERS FROM AMERICAN FAST FOOD RESTAURANTS.

IT IS NOT EASY TO EFFECT GENUINE CHANGE OVER SO LARGE A COUNTRY.

YAO BU YAO SHANG YAN?

YAO.

THE MONKS CARRY PICTURE CELL PHONES.

CHINA'S CURRENT POPULATION IS OVER 1.4 BILLION, THE RECORDS SAY.

BUT BECAUSE UNTOLD NUMBERS OF RURAL FARMERS LIE ABOUT THE NUMBER OF CHILDREN THEY HAVE PRODUCED, THE ACTUAL TOTAL MAY BE MUCH HIGHER.

FSST

EH?

IT IS A MAMMOTH COUNTRY.

IT'S ABOUT TO BE CONQUERED.

THE POLITICS OF HEAVEN

NOW I ASK YOU...IN ALL HONESTY--

--IS THERE ANYTHING SO PLEASANT, SO REMARKABLY SATISFYING...

--AS STARTING A WAR AGAINST A COUNTRY THAT HAS DONE YOU NOTHING BUT COURTESY?

YOU SHOULD HEAR THE SCREAMS...IT'S REALLY QUITE SOMETHING.

Three Sisters, Oregon.

I DON'T GET IT.

WE *FOUND* THE VIBRATORY FREQUENCY THAT KILLED THE STARRO VIRUS IN MY OWN SYSTEM...WHY ISN'T IT WORKING ON THE *CITIZENS?*

THE CONQUEROR STRAIN IS MUTATING, FLASH. IT'S LEARNING TO RESIST. IT'S WHY THE JOB OF A VIROLOGIST IS SO DAMN *HARD.*

YOU'D KILL THE CITIZENS BEFORE KILLING THE *SOURCE.*

ALL I KNOW IS THAT HAVING THAT THING INSIDE ME WAS LIKE SWALLOWING CONCENTRATED *HATE.* THE WHOLE THING SEEMED...

...ALMOST *VENGEFUL.*

I FELT IT, TOO.

WE'VE BEEN UNDER STARRO'S THRALL BEFORE. BUT THIS...

...WAS *DIFFERENT.*

I CAN'T IMAGINE WHAT YOU'VE BEEN THROUGH.

BUT THIS IS NO TIME FOR REFLECTION.

...THESE PEOPLE WILL BEGIN DYING.

IT'LL START WITH THE CHILDREN.

IF WE CAN'T REVERSE THE EFFECTS OF THIS PLAGUE, EVEN WITH THE SEMI-SUSPENDED STATE GREEN LANTERN HAS PLACED THE INFECTED IN...

THAT WON'T HAPPEN.

LANTERN? HOW IS OUR VOLUNTEER?

HE SEEMS OKAY SO FAR, SUPERMAN. IT'S J'ONN I'M WORRIED ABOUT.

HE'S NEVER TRIED TO IMPACT HIS MASS INTO SUCH A CONDENSED STATE.

IT'S TAKING BOTH OF US TO KEEP HIS FORM STABLE.

SO, THE IDEA IS TO HAVE J'ONN USE HIS TELEPATHY ON THE VICTIM?

NOT THE VICTIM, FLASH...

He gave me a word of portent.

"GENERAL."

He said, "GENERAL."

GENERAL? COULD HE MEAN EILING-- THE FORMER SHAGGY MAN?

IT COULDN'T BE ZOD...COULD IT?

NO. NOT ZOD.

TUZIK.

THAT BUFFOON OF A DICTATOR? BUT--

WE UNDERESTIMATED HIM ONCE. LET'S STOP MAKING THAT MISTAKE. NOT ALL SUPER-CRIMINALS WEAR A COSTUME.

THE STARRO VIRUS DELIBERATELY ATTACKED FLASH FIRST, THEN, AT THE NEXT OPPORTUNITY, DIANA

MOST OF OUR ENEMIES TRY TO ELIMINATE SUPERMAN FIRST. YOU WERE BOTH SPECIFICALLY TARGETED.

OF ALL OF US, YOU WERE THE TWO WHO PUT YOUR HANDS ON HIM.

THEY LOVE LOVE **LOVE** US.

CHILDREN. WE ASK THAT YOU STAY IN **LINE.** YOU WILL BE GIVEN A *PAINLESS INOCULATION,* AND THEN YOU WILL BE FED.

DO NOT **FEAR.** WE'RE HERE TO **HELP.**

IT'S...IT'S BEAUTIFUL, ERICH. SOLDAT, I MEAN. IT'S WHAT WE'VE ALWAYS HOPED FOR.

MAKING A REAL CHANGE...HELPING **THOUSANDS.**

MAYBE *MILLIONS. MILLIONS* OF LIVES, SOLDAT!

YES.

IT'S...

WHY AM I NOT HAPPY?

YOU'VE GOT A LUMP THERE, ERICH. DO YOU HAVE A HEADACHE?

I KEEP... I KEEP *THINKING* OF SOMETHING.

PARASITES. VERMIN.

DEATH.

Beijing.

...REMIND YOU THAT YOU ARE A DIPLOMATIC GUEST AND THAT USE OF ANY ALLEGED "POWERS" YOU MAY HAVE WILL BE CONSIDERED A HOSTILE ACT, SUPERMAN.

UNDERSTOOD, MR. LI.

THEN MAY I PRESENT MR. DENG CHUNYAN, CHAIRMEN OF THE STANDING COMMITTEE OF THE POLITICAL BUREAU OF THE COMMUNIST PARTY OF CHINA, CENTRAL COMMITTEE.

I KNOW WHY YOU'RE HERE, SUPERMAN.

YOU ARE NOT WELCOME. I CANNOT STRESS THIS CLEARLY ENOUGH.

IF YOU ENTER CHINESE AIRSPACE UNINVITED, THERE WILL BE GRAVE REPERCUSSIONS.

MR. CHAIRMAN, WITH ALL DUE RESPECT, MY COLLEAGUES HAVE UNDENIABLE PROOF THAT AS WE *SPEAK*, YOUR MILITARY IS BEING APPROPRIATED BY...

"UNDENIABLE?"

WHAT AN ODD CHOICE OF WORDS.

IT IS *QUITE* POSSIBLE TO DENY EVEN THE MOST SEEMINGLY INCONTROVERTIBLE OF "FACTS."

I'VE SEEN THIS BEFORE.

MR. CHAIRMAN...IF THIS VIRUS IS LOOSE, YOU WILL LOSE *EVERYTHING* AND *EVERYONE*.

IGNORE OUR BORDERS AT YOUR PERIL, SUPERMAN. *AND* THAT OF YOUR *COUNTRY*.

GOOD DAY.

WILLFUL, ANGRY IGNORANCE. FEAR OF LOSING EVEN A PIECE OF AN IRON GRIP.

NO GOOD, BATMAN. THERE'S RED TAPE *AROUND* THE RED TAPE HERE.

KEEP TRYING, SUPERMAN. YOU'RE OUR *ONE CHANCE* OF AVOIDING AN INTERNATIONAL INCIDENT THAT COULD DESTROY THE JLA.

HEY, WHY SEND SUPERMAN... ISN'T *DIANA* THE ONE WHO'S GOOD AT THIS POLITICAL STUFF?

DIANA'S AN OFFICIAL U.N. AMBASSADOR. THEMYSCIRA DOESN'T NEED TO ANTAGONIZE CHINA. THEY HAVE PROBLEMS OF THEIR OWN.

BESIDES...

I'M BEING BEATEN TO A BLOODY PULP.

MY LEFT ARM IS INCAPACITATED, AND THANKS TO A DECEPTIVELY GENTLE BLOW TO MY CRANIUM, MY SENSE OF BALANCE IS DUBIOUS AT BEST.

THIS COULD WELL BE MY LAST HAND-TO-HAND COMBAT.

NO REASON TO SHIRK MY DUTY.

LIKE ALL WARS, MARTIAL COMBAT IS ONLY PART OF THIS BATTLE.

A PLAYER HAS TO SET THESE EVENTS IN MOTION.

TUZIK.

HE'S BEEN AHEAD OF US THE WHOLE TIME. IT'S NOT AN APPROACH WE'RE USED TO.

HE'S ATTACKED US AS A GENERAL, WITH AN ALL-OUT MILITARY ASSAULT.

THIS ISN'T SOME GRINNING IDIOT IN A CAPE.

AND HE'S ATTACKED US ON SEVERAL FRONTS...

PROPAGANDA.

BIOLOGICAL.

CHEMICAL.

DIRECT MILITARY FORCE.

AND WORST OF ALL, PERHAPS, HE'S RAISED A HALF-DOZEN INCREDIBLY POWERFUL METAHUMANS--

--INCLUDING THE CHINESE WOMAN WHO IS ATTEMPTING TO CRUSH MY TRACHEA THIS VERY MOMENT.

ALL RIGHT, GENERAL--

--LET'S PLAY.

Three Sisters,
Oregon.

BLAMM!
BLAMM!

DR. FAULKNER.

THE KIDS IN STASIS... THEY'RE *LOOSE.*

YOU'D BETTER COME *RIGHT AWAY!*

China.

J'ONN, IT'S THE CONQUEROR STRAIN. IT'S MUTATED AGAIN--IT'S FOUND A WAY, A FREQUENCY OF SOME SORT...

ONE MOMENT, DR. FAULKNER.

CONTINUE, PLEASE.

IT'S NOW IMMUNE TO THE STASIS FIELD, PERHAPS EVEN TO GREEN LANTERN'S RING ENTIRELY.

THE PRESIDENT HAS SENT AN EVAC ORDER TO ALL MEDICAL AND SCIENCE PERSONNEL.

J'ONN, THEY'RE GOING TO *BOMB* THE AREA.

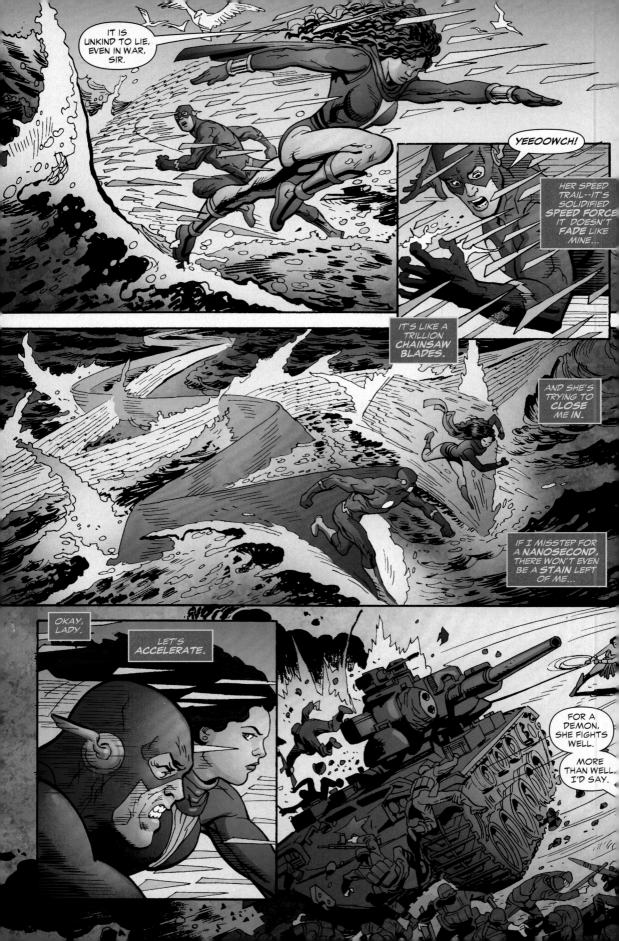

COME ON, WALLY.

YOU KNOW SPEED COMBAT. YOU CAN WIN THIS.

THINK.

UNNNN.

YOU CAN'T BEAT ME, BATMAN.

I CONTAIN ALL THE KNOWLEDGE OF ALL THE GREAT MASTERS OF ALL THE GREAT MARTIAL ARTS FORMS.

PERHAPS NOT.

NO MAN CAN COMPETE WITH THAT. THERE IS NO SHAME IN LOSING TO ME.

BUT I'M PART OF SOMETHING BIGGER THAN JUST MYSELF, JIN SI.

"BUT I COME BACK BECAUSE I KNOW, AT ITS HEART, THAT IT'S GOOD--THAT IT'S MEANINGFUL.

IF I WERE YOU GUYS--

INCREDIBLE. SHE STILL BREATHES.

I COULD DROWN HER. FILL HER LUNGS WITH SALT WATER, PERHAPS?

SEEMS AN UNFAIR DEATH FOR SUCH A WARRIOR.

"WE'RE MORE THAN INDIVIDUALS JIN SI. THAT'S WH' WE'LL WIN.

"I'LL ADMIT I'VE QUESTIONED MY ROLE IN IT.

"I'VE LEFT MORE THAN ONCE.

WE CALL IT THE FOX DEFENSE.

CAN HE DO THAT WITH **ALL** THESE PEOPLE, NOT TO MENTION THE INFECTED IN THE U.S.?

DUNNO, BUT WE'RE GONNA NEED A HUGE THING OF WASABI.

"MR. PRESIDENT, A BIOLOGICAL SOLUTION IS **IMMINENT**. REPEAT, **IMMINENT**..."

...YOU **HAVE** TO CALL BACK THE **FIGHTER PLANES**, SIR.

...MY ADVISORS HAVE TOLD ME THAT THERE'S A 70% CHANCE YOU'RE INFECTED, SUPERMAN.

THAT YOU'RE UNDER THE CONTROL OF THAT ALIEN.

YOUR ADVISORS ARE **WRONG**, MR. PRESIDENT.

I GIVE YOU MY WORD AS AN **AMERICAN**.

BETTER OATH IT UP, LANTERN. J'ONN GOT TUZIK'S **LOCATION** FROM THOSE METAS...LORD KNOWS **WHAT** HE'S GOT IN MIND.

YEAH...ACTUALLY, I HAVE A LITTLE CHORE TO DO, BUT I'LL CATCH RIGHT UP.

SLACKER.

YOU TAKE CARE, TOO, WALLY.

EXCUSE ME. WE ARE... WE **WERE** FREEDOM FIGHTERS.

TUZIK **MURDERED** US, AND THEN HE GAVE US BACK OUR "LIVES" ONLY TO MAKE US **SLAVES**.

PLEASE. LET US **HELP**.

IMPOSSIBLE. I HAD ALL THE... POTIONS... CHECKED.

YES.

BUT I *LIED*, GENERAL.

CHEN DELIVERED... THE RESULTS TO ME... *HIMSELF!*

ARRRRRRRHHH!

I'LL *MANGLE* YOU!

ALL OF YOU!

YOU WILL *NOT!*

...AZIR? SON?

YOU ARE GENERAL *DVORY TUZIK.*

AND YOU *WILL* SHOW DIGNITY IN *DEFEAT* AS YOU *NEVER* DID IN *VICTORY.*

I WILL *NOT* HAVE YOUR LEGACY BE THAT OF A *DROOLING, PETULANT CHILD!*

PLEASE... BRING... BRING ME OVER TO THEM.

YES, MY LADY.

IS THERE *NOTHING* WE CAN DO?

I'M AFRAID THIS IS... NO LONGER OUR RESPONSIBILITY, DIANA.

YOU LOOK HAPPY.

YEAH. I AM.

LOOK, I KNOW I LOST IT A LITTLE BIT ON THIS MISSION. I KNOW I PUT OUR REPUTATIONS ON THE LINE.

AND I KNOW IT COULD'VE ALL ENDED *BAD*.

BUT I'LL BE HONEST.

I'D FIGHT *TEN* ARMIES--

--JUST TO BE HERE AT THIS MOMENT.

MY PEOPLE.

YOU HAVE GIVEN YOUR TRUST TO ME.

I DO NOT YET KNOW IF I HAVE EARNED IT.

I DO NOT YET KNOW IF I DESERVE IT.

BUT IT IS MY WISH...IT IS MY HOPE--

--THAT I WILL MAKE YOU ALL PROUD.

HOW DID YOUR FIRST PRESIDENTIAL ADDRESS FEEL, AZIR?

VAGUELY TERRIFYING. SUPERMAN--

YES?

IT IS... A DEBT NOT EASILY REPAID, OFFERING YOUR LIVES FOR OURS.

TRUTHFULLY, AZIR...YOU AND YOUR COUNTRY-- --YOU REMINDED US WHERE OUR MISSION *SHOULD* BE.

IT'S GIVEN US HOPE THAT WE CAN STILL MAKE THE RIGHT CHOICES, NO MATTER THE COST.

SPEAKING OF HOPE...

...THIS IS FOR YOU, MR. PRESIDENT.

AS A REMEMBRANCE, AND PERHAPS, A REMINDER TO RULE THROUGH TRUTH. *ALWAYS* TRUTH.

MY GOD.

IT'S A LASSO, AZIR. A CORD MADE OF HAIR PLUCKED FROM THE HEADS OF *MANY* AMAZONS.

I BRAIDED IT MYSELF.

EVERY LEADER NEEDS A SYMBOL. SOMETHING TO REMIND THEM OF THEIR *RESPONDIBILTY.*

BE WORTHY OF IT, MR. PRESIDENT.

THAT IS *MY* HOPE.